THIS BOOK BELONGS TO:

- - - - - - - - - - - - - - - - - -

To Christy, my fearless Mama Bear.

As Strong as the River © Flying Eye Books 2020.

First edition published in 2020 by Flying Eye Books,
an imprint of Nobrow Ltd. 27 Westgate Street, London, E8 3RL.

Text and Illustrations © Sarah Noble 2020.

Sarah Noble has asserted her right under the Copyright, Designs and Patents Act,
1988, to be identified as the Author and Illustrator of this Work.

1 3 5 7 9 10 8 6 4 2

Published in the US by Nobrow (US) INC.
Printed in Poland on FSC® certified paper.

ISBN: 978-1-83874-017-7
www.flyingeyebooks.com

SARAH NOBLE

AS STRONG AS THE RIVER

FLYING EYE BOOKS

London | New York

My friends are **BIG**.

I'm big, too.

Though Mama **DISAGREES**.

She says I will grow big someday...

...maybe even bigger than her.

But she says not to hurry.

One day I will be the **BIGGEST** and **STRONGEST** bear.
Everyone knows, there's nothing bigger or stronger than bears.

Mama disagrees.

She says there is something that is **MUCH** bigger and **MUCH** stronger than bears.

The river may be strong, but so am I.

I can cross without even getting wet.

Mama is the best at catching fish.

I'm pretty good at it, too.

These things get passed on, you see.

I fish with all my strength,
because strength is the key to fishing.

Mama disagrees. She says the real key is **PATIENCE**.

WOW! Patience really does pay off!

After a long day's work, me and Mama like to find our special backscratching tree. It scratches even the **ITCHIEST** of itches.

Mama says the river helps to make our tree strong.
Strong enough to hold two big bears.

The river makes lots of things strong, she says.

The river is big, and it is strong.
But the river is also beautiful.

Mama **AGREES**.

I tell Mama she's just like the river...

She's **BIG**,
and **STRONG**,
and **BEAUTIFUL**, too.

And so am I.
Because these things get passed on, you see.